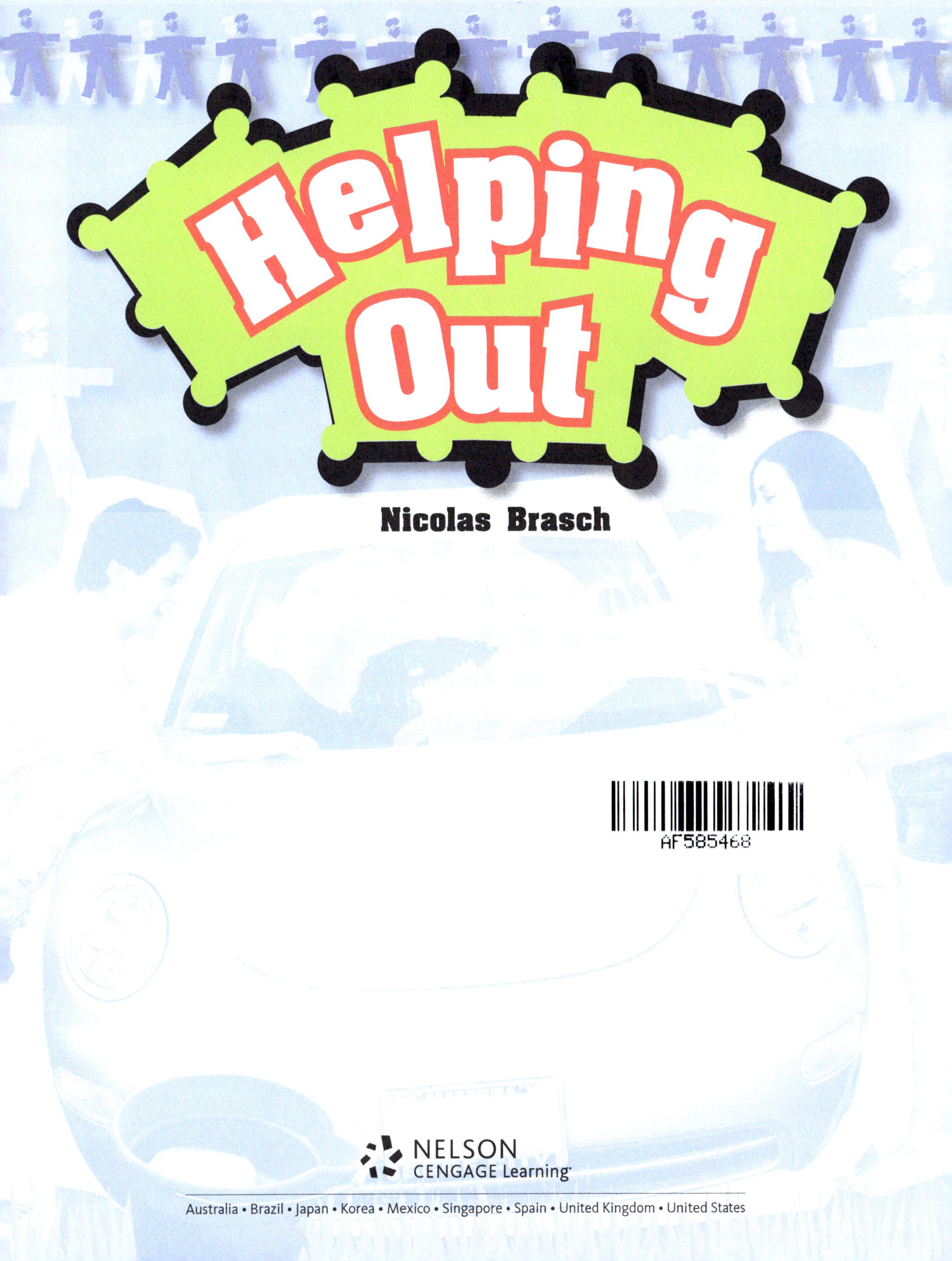

Helping Out

Nicolas Brasch

NELSON
CENGAGE Learning

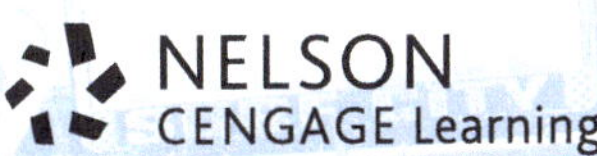

Australia • Brazil • Japan • Korea • Mexico • Singapore • Spain • United Kingdom • United States

Helping Out

Fast Forward

Turquoise Level 17

Text: Nicolas Brasch
Editor: Johanna Rohan
Design: Vonda Pestana
Series design: James Lowe
Production controller: Seona Galbally
Photo research: Corrina Tauschke / Vonda Pestana
Audio recordings: Juliet Hill, Picture Start
Spoken by: Matthew King and Abbe Holmes

Acknowledgements

The author and publisher would like to acknowledge permission to reproduce material from the following sources: Photographs by AAP Image/AP Photo/Rafiq Maqbool, p21; AAP Image/EPA/Barbara Walton, p22; AAP Image/Mick Tsikas, pp 20, back cover; Alamy/Blend Images/Ronnie Kaufman, pp front cover, 1, 10; Alamy/Brand X Pictures/Rob Melnychuk, p11 top; Alamy/OnRequest Images, Inc/Charlie Schuck, p13; Alamy/Paul Doyle, p23; Alamy/Stock Image Pixland/Jerome Tisne, p9; Alamy/thislife pictures, p8; Getty Images/George Doyle, p. 15; Getty Images/George Doyle & Ciaran Griffin, p7 left; Getty Images/Image Source, p19 right; Getty Images/Medio Images, p4 left; Getty Images/Monica Lau, p14 centre; Getty Images/Riser/Frank Herholdt, p5; Getty Images/Taxi, p6; Getty Images/Time Life Pictures, p18; iStockphoto.com, p17 top left; iStockphoto.com/Nicole Weiss, p7 right; iStockphoto.com/Christine Villarin-Jarina, p14 bottom; iStockphoto.com/Cristian Lupu, p23; iStockphoto.com/Daniel Lemay, p11 bottom left; iStockphoto.com/H.L. Hussmann, pp front cover bottom, 1 bottom, 10 bottom; iStockphoto.com/Jonathan Barnes, p4 bottom; iStockphoto.com/Melissa Carroll, p6 inset; iStockphoto.com/Nicholas Morley, p9 centre; iStockphoto.com/Paul Cowan, pp 17 centre left, 19 left; iStockphoto.com/Paul Senyszyn, pp 12-13; iStockphoto.com/Pauline Vos, p23; iStockphoto.com/Ryan Kelly, p14 left; iStockphoto.com/Scott Williams, p11 bottom right; iStockphoto.com/Stan Rohrer, p4 right; NewsPhotos/Tim Hester, p19 bottom right;

ISBN 978 0 17 012628 1
ISBN 978 0 17 012621 2 (set)

Cengage Learning Australia
Level 7, 80 Dorcas Street
South Melbourne, Victoria Australia 3205
Phone: 1300 790 853

Cengage Learning New Zealand
Unit 4B Rosedale Office Park
331 Rosedale Road, Albany, North Shore NZ 0632
Phone: 0800 449 725

For learning solutions, visit **cengage.com.au**

Printed in Australia by Ligare Pty Ltd
6 7 8 9 10 11 12 20 19 18 17 16

THE UNIVERSITY OF MELBOURNE

Evaluated in independent research by staff from the Department of Language, Literacy and Arts Education at the University of Melbourne.

Helping Out

Nicolas Brasch

Contents

Chapter 1

UNPAID WORK

Unpaid work is work that people do without getting paid for it.

Everybody does unpaid work. Mowing the grass, ironing clothes and cleaning the kitchen are all examples of unpaid work.

Even people who have a paid job do unpaid work.

Communities couldn't operate if people didn't do unpaid work. A lot of **needy people** wouldn't get help. This is because communities can't afford to pay people to do all the jobs that are needed.

Even a household couldn't operate if people didn't do unpaid work – like vacuuming the carpet!

Chapter 2

HOME DUTIES

Home duties are unpaid jobs that are done at home.

Looking after young children is an example of a home duty.
In some homes,
the person who stays home with young children has to stop doing paid work.

Home duties also involve tasks like cleaning the house, washing the car and mowing the lawn.

Some households pay someone
to do these tasks for them.
But, in most households,
people don't have enough money to pay other people
to do their home duties.

Running Words 172

Chapter 3

CARERS

Carers are people who care for other people. The people they care for need special help. It may be because they are elderly.

It may be because they have had an accident
or have a medical condition.
It may be because they live alone
and just want some company.

Many carers care for someone in their own family.
They might care for their parents when their parents can no longer look after themselves.
Or, they might look after their nieces or nephews.

Many grandparents look after their grandchildren during the day.
This is so both of the children's parents can go to work and earn an **income**.

Some carers choose to care for people who are not members of their family. These carers just want to help people in need.

By doing this, they are also helping the family of the person being cared for. This is because the family doesn't have to find the money to **hire** a paid worker to help the person in need.

The carer is also helping the community.
This is because the community
doesn't have to find the money
to pay for someone to help the person in need.

Chapter 4

VOLUNTEERS

Volunteers are people who do a job for the satisfaction of helping others.

Volunteers do many different types of jobs. Some volunteers read books onto tapes so that people with poor eyesight can listen.

Some volunteers deliver meals to elderly or sick people.

Some volunteers help tourists who visit a city during a major event like the Olympic Games or the Commonwealth Games.

Volunteers help whenever a community is hit by a natural disaster.
Volunteers assist in putting out bush fires.
They might also help to evacuate people from areas that have been flooded or hit by an earthquake or tsunami.

A community may not recover without the help of volunteers.

Some communities require volunteers more than others. Communities that don't have much money require a great deal of help from volunteers.

Communities with a large number of elderly people might require more help from volunteers than communities with more young people. Without volunteers, some communities couldn't operate.

Glossary

hire	to employ someone
income	money received for work
needy people	people who need help

Index